D1622388

THE MAYHEM ON
MOHAWK AVENUE

Darby Creek
A division of Lerner Publishing Group, Inc.
241 First Avenue North
Minneapolis, MN 55401 U.S.A.

Website address: www.lernerbooks.com

Cover and interior photographs © Eco Images/
Universal Images Group/Getty Images
(neighborhood); © iStockphoto.com/appletat
(silhouette).

Main body text set in Janson Text LT Std 12/17.5.
Typeface provided by Adobe Systems.

———————

Library of Congress
Cataloging-in-Publication Data

Atwood, Megan.
     The mayhem on Mohawk Avenue / by Megan
Atwood.
        p.   cm. — (The paranormalists ; case #03)
     Summary: High schoolers Jinx and Jackson
investigate a new student's claim that ghosts are
following him.
     ISBN 978-0-7613-8334-5 (lib. bdg. : alk.
paper)
        [1. Ghosts—Fiction. 2. Supernatural—Fiction.
3. Best friends—Fiction. 4. Friendship—Fiction.]
I. Title.
PZ7.A8952 May 2012
[Fic]—dc23   2011047664

Manufactured in the United States of America
1 – PP –7/15/12

THE PARANORMALISTS
CASE#3

THE MAYHEM ON
MOHAWK AVENUE

MEGAN ATWOOD

darbycreek
MINNEAPOLIS

THE PARANORMALISTS

INVESTIGATION #02:
BLACK EAGLE TAVERN

Investigation two turned into our best yet, Paranormalist Fans. If you ever doubted the existence of ghosts . . . well, this nightmare in food service proves you wrong. I approach all cases with skepticism, PFs, and I make sure there is evidence to back up any supernatural claims. I mean, I have the equipment! And the equipment doesn't lie. There is indisputable evidence that a ghost inhabited the place. Although the fact that I almost died during our last case convinced me more than the EVP readings that this ghost was real.

Here's how it came about: Subject came to the investigation team claiming his parents' business was haunted. Subject had corroborating stories from clients of the business. Upon interviewing them, the investigation team confirmed that the stories were authentic, for sure. And that corroborating witnesses had really good tea.

Anyway, the case sounded compelling, PFs. Bottles flying, voices talking . . . Everyone more than a little scared. Evidently this place was always haunted, but the spirit had been nice. He'd turned mean, it seemed. So Investigator #2 and I spent one night there, and guess what happened?

Nothing.

Per usual, I was suspicious. After our case with the hoaxer, I thought maybe we were being played again. But subject was so nice and seemed genuinely upset and also had great hair. So we dug a little deeper and found something else out—the activity really only happened when subject's brother was on the premises too. The plot thickened!

So we stayed the night again, this time with the brothers. And PFs, I am not exaggerating when I say I thought I might be killed. Bottle after bottle smashed against the wall, glasses flew off the shelves, the place shook, and the lights went out. Investigation team's equipment went crazy with readings.

This was one angry ghost.

It turns out the spirit was being aggravated by the brothers' fighting. And we were in the crossfire.

Long story short, the brothers found a way to make peace. And so did our angry spirit. We decided to let the dead lie, so to speak.

The Rundown on the Black Eagle Tavern:

EVP: Voices captured. Audible phrases include the following: "Lissssten . . ." (I KNOW! Creepy, right?)

EMF: Crazy activity. Needle on red the whole time.

Video: Showed lights going out, but no bottles or anything thrown because there is no night vision on the recording device. Or infrared. Sigh. I need one of those cameras.

Temperature: Dropped many degrees.

Verdict: MAJORLY HAUNTED. See video channel from the client for testimonial.

So on to our next adventure, PFs! What do you think the otherworld has in store for us? Comment below, and as always, remember that the Paranormalists SEEK THE TRUTH AND FIND THE CAUSE!

CHAPTER 1

Jinx fired up her computer, excited to respond to the Paranormalists fan who had asked for help with a house haunting. This could be the start of something spectacular! It was exactly what she had wanted—the Paranormalists' reputation was bringing in clients. And not even from her high school! Her wish had been granted by a reader who called him- or herself Mayhem on Mohawk Ave. She clicked on her e-mail and wrote back, careful to sound enthusiastic but not desperate.

Dear Mayhem,

Thanks for writing. We Paranormalists would love to help—it's what we live for! Can you be more specific about what types of supernatural activity you've noticed? We have a lot of experience and can help in a lot of different ways. Do you want to banish the ghosts too?

We can talk more about rate after we figure out exactly what is needed. Do you want to meet with the Paranomalist team at a coffee shop in town and chat?

Remember, Paranormalists SEEK THE TRUTH AND FIND THE CAUSE. We're here for you.

Sincerely,

Jinx - Paranormalist Investigation Team

Jinx reread what she wrote, then pressed send with a flourish. Her first Internet client! Things were shaping up. After the last case, Jinx couldn't help but feel a little shaky, but more determined than ever to investigate more hauntings. She'd started the website and the investigations just to get some notoriety, but she found out fast how much she loved everything about ghost hunting. The equipment, the weird cases, the questions they brought up, and especially working with her best friend, Jackson. She wasn't quite sure why he was into it so much, but it didn't matter— they were in it together.

Plus, she was good at it. Really good.

After years of not standing out in anything, finally Jinx had found the thing that made her the best. And she loved it.

She glanced at the clock on her iPhone. Jackson would be there any minute to pick her up for school, and he always hated it when she was late. Which was always. She couldn't wait to tell him about the e-mail she'd sent, so she sprinted down the stairs and grabbed her coat and backpack to wait outside for him. She was practically humming with energy.

Just as her hand closed on the doorknob, her mom poked her head out of the kitchen and yelled, "Jane. Breakfast."

Jinx rolled her eyes as she jogged into

the kitchen. "I told you to call me Jinx, Mom." Jinx grabbed a pack of Twizzlers off the counter and turned to walk away. Her mom took the candy from her hands as Jinx walked past and said, eyebrows raised, "A real breakfast."

Jinx sighed. She grabbed a banana from the stand and held it up for her mom's inspection. Her mom sighed back, "I guess." She set her coffee cup in the sink. "Better than nothing. What's the hurry anyway? Jackson's not here yet."

Jinx gave her mom a big grin. "I just love school so much." Her mom laughed. Jinx noticed she was extra dressed up. She wore a suit with a skirt and heels. Her mom *never* wore heels. "What's with the outfit?" Jinx asked, her mouth full of banana.

Her mom gave a big smile. "Interview today for VP. How do I look?"

Jinx shrugged. "Like a mom."

"I guess that's good," her mom said. Just then, Jinx heard the honk that meant Jackson had arrived.

She threw the banana peel on the counter and yelled back, "Good luck" as she ran out the door.

Jumping into Jackson's car, Jinx bounced on the seat and slammed the door.

"Careful! Watch it," Jackson said.

Jinx rolled her eyes for the second time that morning. "I forgot about your car's delicate nature."

Jackson grinned and patted the dashboard. "You mean Bertha. Bertha's done me well, so you should treat her with respect."

"Blah blah. Guess what? I wrote that dude back. We may have our fifth case soon."

Jackson snorted. "You mean third. You're not counting those first two with just the two of us? Because those were . . ."

Jinx finished the sentence. "Amateur, I know. But they got us to where we are, didn't they?"

"I was going to say 'ridiculous,'" Jackson said. "Since, you know, we are still ghost-hunting amateurs."

Jinx shook her head. "We're professionals! We charge."

Jackson snorted. "You charge."

"Whatever. Anyway, we need to gear up and see what happens with this guy. I'm hoping we'll get more requests online—maybe we could even go international!"

Jackson rounded into the school parking lot and found a spot as far from the school as possible. Jinx hated it—he insisted that walking was good for them, so he parked far away from everything. But since he was picking Jinx up every day, it's not like she could complain.

"You mean, like *Ghost Hunters*?"

Jinx got out of the car and slung her backpack on her shoulders. "Yes! And I know Portland isn't exactly Hollywood, but maybe we could have a *teen* show about ghost hunting? Wouldn't that be awesome?"

Jackson shook his head as they walked toward the school. "This is one e-mail, J. One."

"No, it's the *start*, Jackson," Jinx said, walking through the main doors. "It's our beginning."

Then she stopped short. So short, Jackson ran into her.

There on the bulletin board, just inside the school doors, was Jinx's worst nightmare.

A dark, shiny poster full of amazing graphics was spread across most of the board, crowding out school lunch menus and events calendars.

It read:

NEED TO BANISH A GHOST?
CALL THE EXPERT:
THE PARANORMALATOR.
I SEEK KNOWLEDGE
AND FIND THE SOURCE.
**Call 555-GHOST,
OR VISIT ME ONLINE!**

Jackson and Jinx looked at each other. Jinx's mouth hung wide open. Everything about the poster ripped off the Paranormalists. All of Jinx's hard work on the website, all of the equipment she saved up to buy . . . and here someone had completely copied everything she and Jackson had done! And somehow managed to advertise at school!

Someone will die for this, was all Jinx could think.

CHAPTER 2

After ripping the poster down despite Jackson's protests, Jinx marched into the front office to confront the school secretary.

Brandishing the poster like a weapon, Jinx yelled, "How did this person post this?"

The secretary, a recent college graduate who obviously hated his job, turned away from his laptop screen and looked at Jinx with bored eyes. "Can I help you?"

Jinx shook the poster. "This!" was all she

could say. Jackson, who had followed her into the office, took over.

"We're just wondering if this poster was approved before it was put up on the bulletin board."

In a slow voice, the secretary said, "I doubt it."

Jinx whinnied with impatience. "Who put it up there?"

The secretary shrugged his shoulders. "How should I know?"

Before Jinx could respond the way she wanted to (it involved a few swear words), Jackson grabbed her sleeve and pulled her out of the office.

"Jinx," he said, "that obviously wasn't going to work. And anyway, who cares if some person is copying us? We're clearly the better outfit around here. Otherwise, why would they have to copy?"

Jinx flipped around and drilled her eyes into Jackson. "Who cares?" She could feel a vein pulsing in her forehead. "*I care.*" Her eyes narrowed. "And I'm going to find out who put up that poster."

She stormed down the hall to her locker. Jackson might not care, she thought, but Jinx's whole life was wrapped up in the website. No way was some poser going to interrupt her dreams.

She reached her locker and flipped the dial. She couldn't even see straight. The first two tries at opening the locker failed. Finally, she got the right combination and lifted the handle. Grabbing her Algebra II book, she prepared to slam the locker shut but then overheard a conversation right next to her.

An obvious-freshman boy with red hair and freckles was talking to an equally obvious-freshman girl. If Jinx hadn't been so angry, she would have giggled about how the boy also obviously had a crush on the girl. But the words coming out of his mouth made her see red.

"Yeah, he's got family on the *Ghost Hunters* crew, so he knows all about that stuff. He's stayed in some pretty scary places. He's got a blog and everything."

The girl shivered. "I don't know who would want to hunt ghosts. But he still sounds pretty cool."

The boy puffed out his chest. "I'd do it. I'm totally not scared about that sort of stuff. I'm not sure I even believe in it. But this guy says he's moved all over the country following the *Ghost Hunters* team. He says his dad is on the production crew. Anyway, that's why he moved here. His folks got a place on Mohawk Avenue, I think."

Jinx slammed her locker shut. Time to make some freshman talk.

"Hey, you!" She pointed at the boy, and he stepped back like she had slapped him.

He mouthed, "Me?"

Jinx raised her eyebrows and nodded. "Yeah, I mean you." The girl stared wide-eyed at Jinx.

"Y-y-yeah?" The boy swallowed audibly.

"Who's this dude you're talking about?"

The redheaded boy said, "His name is Brian. He's a junior."

The freshman girl's face lit up as she was staring at Jinx. "Hey! Aren't you that spooky girl who has a ghost-hunting website too?"

Jinx turned her full glare on the girl.

"Too? Brian the poser copied *me*. And yeah, I'm that spooky girl."

The boy smiled a not-especially-kind smile at Jinx. "Looks like you've got some competition."

Jinx stepped up to the boy until their noses almost touched. Jinx was only five-four, but the kid was about her height, too. He was so surprised, he stumbled backwards. She followed him until he ran into the wall of lockers.

Turning on her heel, she flipped around and walked down the hall. She heard the girl say, "Oh my god, that girl is sooooo creepy."

Jinx smiled to herself. Just what she was aiming for.

Now all she had to do was find this Brian and let him know what he had coming.

CH**3**APTER

Jackson looked down the street for the billionth time and made sure his phone was off. No one was around that he knew. He could go in. What was the big deal, anyway? He was a paranormal investigator—who would question him going into the store? The thoughts didn't make him feel any better.

The Eye of Ra Metaphysical Shop was near a local college campus. So his *biggest* problem would be seeing one of his brothers on this street. With one last glance around, he opened the door to the shop.

A bell chimed as he walked into the store, and immediately Jackson's nose was filled with incense. Lots and lots of incense. When he walked back out, he'd smell like a Tibetan ashram.

Oh well, he thought. *It'll make Mom happy I don't smell like sweat for once.*

He had bought crystals at the shop before, special ones designed for ghost banishings, but he hadn't had a chance to use them. He wasn't one hundred percent sure they would work. In fact, after reading some of the stuff in the shop, he wasn't thirty percent sure they would work. But what was the harm? Anyway, this day he was in the shop for a different reason. A much different reason. And this reason made him incredibly nervous.

He turned around and almost ran into a salesperson. Jackson jumped back and bumped into some astrology books, knocking down a display. The salesperson, wearing exactly what Jackson thought a shopkeeper at a place

called The Eye of Ra should wear—a long,
flowing skirt and tunic—smiled while Jackson
apologized profusely. She and Jackson began
picking up books.

"I'm so sorry," Jackson said one more time
as he placed the last fallen book on the holder.
"Just didn't see you there."

The shopkeeper beamed a radiant smile
at him. "My dear, it seems we were meant to
bump into each other."

Jackson fought hard not to roll his eyes. He
was glad Jinx wasn't around. She wouldn't have
lasted a second with this woman.

The shopkeeper looked at him with wide
blue eyes. "Are you seeking something in
particular?"

Jackson was taken aback by the question.
The word *seeking* had taken on a new meaning
lately. Yes, he was seeking something. And he
needed one tool to get it. Or so he hoped.

He cleared his throat. "Well, I'm looking
for a . . . Ouija board."

The woman leaned in. "A what, dear?"

Jackson said it more loudly—so loudly

a customer in the back turned to him and glared. "A Ouija board."

"Oh." The shopkeeper leaned back. Disappointment washed over her features. "Oh. Having a slumber party, are we? You seem a little old for that . . . At any rate, they are called spirit boards now, dear. The connotations of the old name have been so awful, they've renamed them. Though like many things, the problem is not with the boards, but with the people who use them."

She sniffed the air, then pointed listlessly to the back of the room. "Over there. We get our largest sales around Halloween, but I suppose you're simply getting a jump on things, eh?"

Then she turned around and drifted down another aisle.

Jackson felt the urge to explain himself. But instead he went to the back of the store and began looking at the spirit boards.

He didn't realize there were so many kinds. He could get a witchcraft one, a hexagonal one, a simple, no-frills one, a glow-in-the-dark one, one with dice, one with cards . . . he just didn't know what to choose. He glanced back at the shopkeeper and then squared his shoulders. He'd ask, even though she clearly thought the boards were an embarrassment.

He walked toward shelf of crystals she was dusting and said, "I don't know which one to get."

She waved her hand and didn't look at him. "Oh, any of them will do for your purposes, I'm sure."

Jackson cleared his throat again. "Actually . . . I'm not doing this with a friend. I want to contact . . ." He swallowed. For some reason, saying it out loud, to another person, made him blush. He had never even told Jinx—he didn't think he ever could. But he continued. "I want to contact my father."

The shopkeeper put her duster down slowly, turning to look Jackson in the eye. Jackson could see pity on the woman's face— something he hated—but also some respect. He didn't mind the last part.

She became all business and led Jackson to the back of the store. "What you'll want is the standard Ouija board," she said, eyes sparkling.

"Glow-in-the-dark has the same arrangement of letters, but really, that's for people who don't take this seriously." She grabbed the plainest board and handed it to Jackson.

He took it and looked it over. After a beat, he asked the question that he most wanted answered. And the one he was most afraid of. "Does it work?"

She stopped in her tracks and looked very seriously at him. "Yes. Sometimes. When the spirits are willing. And if there is a great enough need."

Jackson wasn't concerned about the last part. There was definitely a great enough need. He missed his dad like he would miss an arm. He just wanted one last conversation with him. Maybe some advice on how to be a good man. Advice on anything, really—he just wanted to hear his dad one last time.

After his and Jinx's last case, Jackson knew without a doubt that ghosts existed. And if they did, that meant he had a chance to talk to his father. He had never been as happy as when the ghost at the Black Eagle Tavern threw glasses at the wall. Jackson's hope had reared its head high.

The shopkeeper wasn't done. She put her hand on his arm, and her eyes softened. "But dear, many times a spirit has crossed over and is gone from this place. Completely." Jackson stiffened, but she held tighter to his arm. "And that's a good thing," the woman said softly. "So if you don't receive the response you're looking for . . . it's probably a good sign."

This was not what Jackson wanted to hear. He shrugged off the words. "When is the best time to try for communication?"

She let go of his arm, and her voice became businesslike again. "Midnight. Trite but true. And another trite but true piece of advice: wait for Halloween. Many ancient societies, and many modern ones as well, believe that is the time when the veil between worlds is thinnest."

Jackson nodded. He didn't think he could wait until Halloween. That was almost six weeks away. Maybe he'd give it a try beforehand.

He and the shopkeeper went to the cash register, and Jackson paid for the board. Before he left, she looked him carefully in the eyes. "I wish you luck, dear."

Jackson nodded and felt a lump form in his throat. He walked out of the shop without thinking to look around. As he reached his car, board in hand, someone called out his name.

His head whipped up and turned from side to side. There, jogging toward him, was Haley Richards. Head cheerleader. Jinx's nemesis. Most popular girl in school. Jackson swallowed. *Busted*.

She ran up to him and said, slightly out of breath, "Did you just buy a Ouija board?"

Jackson shrugged awkwardly.

Haley's big green eyes stared at him. "I heard you in the shop."

Jackson started. Haley had been in there? Doing what?

Haley continued. "I was going to buy one, too. I want to contact my grandma." She looked at the ground, and Jackson could see the signs of a blush. "Can we do it together?"

Jackson leaned against the car. *Well*, he thought, *life keeps getting stranger and stranger*.

CHAPTER 4

Haley didn't look Jackson in the eyes, and he knew enough not to say anything that would make her feel bad. So he said the only thing that made sense to him. "Do you want to come over right now and look at it?"

Haley's eyes shone in response. She smiled and nodded. Then, a little bashfully, she said, "I walked here—do you think I could have a ride?"

Another surprise. Jackson knew Haley lived in a wealthy part of town, all the way on the other side. And she had a great car.

As if reading his mind, she said, "I was afraid someone would recognize me or my car."

Jackson chuckled a little. "I know how you feel." He walked to his car's other side and opened the door for her. For some reason, he felt the urge to be chivalrous.

It was only when he turned the key in the ignition that he had the thought: Jinx would be furious.

No, *furious* wasn't a strong enough word. Livid. Horrified. His mind drifted back to a word he'd had to spell in the regional spelling bee when he was in eighth grade: *apoplectic*. Yeah, Jinx wouldn't like this one bit.

He gritted his jaw and backed out of the parking lot. Jinx was his best friend, but even she couldn't understand what it was like to lose someone so important in life. Jackson could see in Haley's eyes that her grandma was precious to her. Maybe he could finally talk about his hope to somehow, in some way, speak with his dad again.

He asked Haley softly, "When did your grandma pass away?"

She answered with tears in her voice. "She passed away two years ago. In the summer."

Silence took over the car for a bit. Then Haley said, "I'm sorry about your dad."

Jackson nodded. After three years, it was still hard to talk about.

Haley went on, "I remember when it happened. No one really knew what to say. We were so young, you know? I kept thinking about you, though. I hope you know that."

The lump was back in Jackson's throat, so he nodded again. To lighten the mood, he said, "So did you pick anything up at the store? Like any incense?"

Haley laughed. "I think I've had enough incense to last me a lifetime, thank you very much."

"So, do you think we should wait for midnight before we try this thing?" Jackson said.

Haley twisted her lip, something that reminded Jackson of Jinx so much he practically felt a punch in the gut. "Hmm," she said. "Maybe. But I don't think my parents would like that too much."

Jackson thought for a minute. "You ever sneak out?"

Haley snorted. "Like, all the time."

Jackson's excitement rose. "Do you think you could sneak over to my house at quarter to midnight? I'll drop you off now, then you can come over and we can try the board."

Haley thought for a minute and then said, "Probably not, actually. You live so far away I'd have to drive, and if my parents woke up and noticed my car gone . . ."

Jackson grinned. "How about I sneak *into* your house instead?"

She grinned back. "That's perfect. Except we should wait until Wednesday, because my dad doesn't work late. I'll draw you a quick map of where my bedroom is. There's a tree just outside my window that I always use to sneak out. It's super easy to get back in, so I don't think you'll have any problems."

Jackson blushed. "Uh, I remember where your room is."

He felt Haley's eyes on him. "Ohhhhhh!" she said. "From the party in seventh grade!"

Jackson nodded and laughed a little. "We had to do seven minutes in your closet."

Haley laughed back. "Yeah, it was more like two and a half. And we were both so scared we didn't even stand next to each other, let alone kiss."

Jackson started laughing harder, and Haley joined in. Soon they had reached Haley's house, and they stopped laughing long enough for Haley to get out.

She stooped back through the car door and looked Jackson straight in the eyes, a smile playing on her lips. "I'll see you Wednesday. Eleven forty-five. And we won't even need the closet this time."

Jackson smiled back.

In fact, he smiled the entire way home.

CHAPTER 5

Jinx's fingers flew over the keyboard.

She'd tried calling, but the number was disconnected.

She *would* find this guy—if it was the last thing she did.

Jackson didn't seem to be answering his phone or any texts—and she had tried both a million times—so it was up to her to figure it out. No one at school could give her a last name for Brian the imposter. Assuming Brian was really his name.

So far, she'd gone through every single post on the Paranormalator's site. Every single one read eerily like the stuff on her and Jackson's site. Nowhere could she find the address of the originator, even after searching for the IP address. This guy was good. In fact, a part of her kind of admired his stealth. Still, why hide his identity if he was bragging at school? Why bother copying her and Jackson at all? Jinx was baffled.

Her next step was to check the names of the crew members on *Ghost Hunters*. There were so many that Jinx went through three packets of Twizzlers before she'd added them to her list. Secretly, she was sort of excited about this part. She had always wanted to know the ins and outs of the show. And she would have to research them one by one to see if any of them had a family that lived in Portland.

In the meantime, though, she'd leave a little trap for this so-called Brian.

She clicked on the "Contact" section on the Paranormalator's site and typed in a message. She loved these types of contact forms—all it would show the Paranormalator was the fake e-mail address Jinx had made— which would forward the reply along to her— and the message she sent:

> *Dear Paranormalator,*
>
> *I'm hoping you can help me. I think my house is haunted, and it's getting really scary. Can you tell me what your rates are and what we can do to get rid of the ghosts?*
>
> *Sincerely,*
>
> *Haley*

Jinx thought that Haley was a good name to use. Why not? She smiled at herself and added the e-mail address she'd whipped up for just that purpose.

Done.

She just had to wait for the reply e-mail to bounce her way. Then she'd set up a meeting. And then pummel this guy.

She clicked open the Paranormalists dashboard and wrote a quick post.

Well, PFs, it looks like our site has its very own copycat. Is it true that imitation is the best form of flattery? If so, well . . . we've been well flattered.

I won't tell you the name of the copycatter, because I have values and I am a nice person. But suffice it to say that we have been ripped off in a BIG way. Right down to the name on our website.

But, my loyal PFs, I know you'll stay faithful to us. Why? Because we are the real deal. We're an inseparable team dedicated to each other and the pursuit of the paranormal. And we report to you from knee-deep in investigations so true, they'll haunt you at nights. Remember, we Paranormalists always SEEK THE TRUTH AND FIND THE CAUSE.

—Investigator #1

Jinx was just about to close her laptop when she heard the ding that meant she had another e-mail. Maybe it was Jackson finally getting back to her. She opened her mail and found she had a message from Mayhem on Mohawk Ave. Finally.

Hi Jinx,

Thanks for writing me back. I'm not ready to meet—I'm sort of hoping this will go away soon—but I may be ready later.

Anyway, things keep flying around my house. It happens only when I'm home and never when my parents are. Is that normal? I just moved here and I'm in the 8th grade, so I don't have a lot of money. But if this doesn't get any better, could I hire you and Investigator #2?

P.S. I love your site. It reminds me a lot of the Paranormalator. Did you know that that guy's dad works on the Ghost Hunters *crew?*

I like your stories better, though, so I want to go with you. Let me know if I can do anything on my own to get this stuff to stop. I'd really appreciate it.

Peace,

Mayhem

Jinx slammed her laptop shut. "Ugh!" she cried to no one. This guy knew about the Paranormalator? Jinx was so irritated she could hardly stand it. She twisted her lip and picked up her phone, dialing Jackson for the millionth time.

Still no answer.

She threw the phone down on her bed and then heard her mother's voice carry up the stairs. "Jane, can you come down here please?"

That voice was her you're-in-trouble voice. And because Jinx rarely did anything too naughty, she knew there could be only reason for the talk: her overnight investigations.

She gulped and heard her mom yell up again, "Jane?" Her little brother chimed in with a singsong voice, "Jaaaneee! Come here!" She would have to kill him later. She made a mental note.

Walking down the stairs as slowly as possible, she tried to think of a way out of the mess. She could say that she had been drugged and kidnapped. Both times. No, that wouldn't work. That she had hit her head and entered a fugue state? Equally bad. That she wasn't really their daughter but an alien cyborg that had snuck out to study nighttime Earth phenomena?

As she reached the end of the stairs, Jinx saw both her mom and dad standing in front of the couch. Her mom had her hands behind her back.

"Jane, it has come to our attention . . . ," her dad began.

Her mother interrupted. "Jinx, honey."

This took Jinx by surprise. Her mom never remembered to call her that.

Her dad hit himself in the head. "That's right. OK, Jinx, it has come to our attention . . ."

Sweat trickled down Jinx's spine, but her mom cut in excitedly, ". . . that you have been accepted into the Junior Scholars program through the U!"

Jinx blinked. Junior Scholars? She hadn't even applied for that. It was some stupid program where you had to take college courses instead of high school courses to get a "head start" in college. And who would want to take harder classes?

Her mom nodded. "I know, I know, you didn't really apply. But I sent in your grades and your standardized scores, and they accepted you! Isn't that great, honey?"

She came over to Jinx, but Jinx stepped away. "Well, no! I didn't apply for a reason." She glared at her mom.

Her mother glanced at her dad, and he nodded. "We were afraid you'd say that. So, we have another nugget of good news that's relevant. You are looking at the new vice president of BriteCorp!"

Jinx blinked again. "Congratulations," she said grudgingly.

Her mom nodded. "It's great for everyone. For instance, I can now get some things for you kids that maybe you've wanted for forever." She looked hard at Jinx. "Like, say, an infrared camera." She flourished a package from behind her back.

Jinx nearly fainted. "You've got to be

kidding me!" she yelled and then made a squealing sound she had no idea she could make. She reached her hands out for it, but before she could grab it, her mom said, "But this is a full-on bribe, Jinx. If you do Junior Scholars, you can have the camera."

Jinx's shoulders slumped. "That's blackmail."

"It sure is!" her dad said cheerily. "But with love."

"Fine, I'll do Junior Scholars," Jinx muttered. Visions of homework swam in her head.

Then her mom handed her the camera, and all was forgotten.

Jinx raced up the stairs, yelling "Thanks!" behind her, ready to rip off the packaging and start trying out the new camera.

But first, she needed to tell Jackson.

She dialed his number again. Straight to voicemail.

She sent a text. *Where r u? I have news.*

After waiting for an excruciating three minutes, she wrote him an e-mail.

Hey dingus,

Where are you? I have awesome news. Also, that Mayhem person who needs our help wrote back, but isn't ready to meet. I'll write back tonight and see if I can't talk them into it. They're only in the 8th grade, though, so we probably won't get paid. But that's OK because that means I get to try out my new equipment! What equipment you ask? You'll just have to wait and see.

Also, I've made some headway on the evil Brian guy and I've set a trap. We may be meeting him soon. More to come.

Waiting waiting waiting

J

Jinx shut her laptop and took one last look at her phone. Jackson always called back within minutes. And he never left a text unanswered. She twisted her lip and wondered whether she should call his mom.

She knew he'd kill her for that, though, so she dismissed the idea. And anyway, she had an awesome camera to look at.

Still, even as she turned out the lights and tried out the new infrared, she wondered, where was Jackson?

C H A P T E R 6

On Wednesdays, Jackson had football meetings in the morning, so Jinx got a ride from her mom. She told herself for the millionth time that she needed her own car.

As she walked to her locker, her iPhone pinged. She scanned the e-mail and a thrill ran through her. It was from the Paranormalator—he'd taken the bait.

Dear Haley,
You chose the right person to write to—

my site is the REAL site to go to when you have a haunting problem. I'd be happy to meet you. I don't know where you are located, but if you are near Jefferson High or if you go there, I'll be at the picnic tables outside the cafeteria at 12:00. You can find me there. Otherwise, let's set up a time to meet.

Remember, the Paranormalator always SEEKS KNOWLEDGE AND FINDS THE SOURCE.

Sincerely,
Brian – Portland's #1 Ghost Hunter

Jinx growled. #1 Ghost Hunter her butt. No way was this guy for real. She shook it off—her plan had worked. She would be able to meet this infamous Brian and tell him off, once and for all.

She looked around for a sign of Jackson, but he still hadn't answered her calls. She was starting to get worried, and getting worried about other people was something Jinx tried hard not to do. So, on top of everything else, she was cranky.

The first bell rang, and she ran to her locker, got out her English book, and groaned. Sitting behind Haley Richards in English was the worst part of her day. Could the girl be any more like something from a bad eighties teen movie? Perfect strawberry-blonde hair, big green eyes, cheerleader . . . basically, the anti-Jinx. And it seemed Haley felt the same way about her. Jinx ran through her zingers on the off chance Haley said something to her.

Girls. No wonder her best friend was a boy.

Jinx drummed her fingers in her history class. The clock was broken; it had to be. No way could time move that slowly. More than once her teacher had asked her to quit fidgeting, but Jinx was pretty sure he'd done something to the clock. Finally, the minute hand clicked to the ten place and the bell rang. Finally. 11:50.

Jinx had to run to her locker to put her things away and to grab her camera. Then she would meet this Brian guy and make him pay.

She still hadn't seen Jackson all day, but they shared sixth period study hall, so she'd quiz him then. She wished they had lunch together so he could watch the showdown in action, but then thought better of it. Jackson was the kind of guy who did things more quietly. He probably wouldn't approve.

Grabbing her camera and her lunch, she raced down the stairs to the cafeteria, hoping to get to the picnic table first. To her surprise, a group of students already huddled around the table, a kid talking in the middle. Jinx could see his huge gestures from where she stood. She was pretty sure it was Brian, but she wanted to be positive. Moving casually in a wide arc around the group of students, she went and stood by some bushes that allowed her to stay in the shadows. She felt a few pricklies here and there, but she could hear everything. She snapped a couple of photos just in case it was indeed the Paranormalator.

". . . knives flying everywhere! So my dad comes down and says, off-camera of course, that if the ghost was such a culinary whiz, why couldn't it be throwing steak tartar?"

The crowd laughed, and Jinx snorted—was

he serious with this crap? She took a good look at him. Skinny, kind of short, black T-shirt, dark hair, black Chucks. Nothing unusual about him except that was he was able to get everyone's attention. Seven kids stood around the table. Narrowing her eyes, Jinx realized they were all freshmen.

Well, that made more sense. No respectable sophomore, junior, or senior would listen to this junk.

Brian continued. "Yeah, so anyway, I'm meeting a client here. It's my fifteenth case, so I'm pretty sure I can help her."

As if on cue, a freshman girl piped up, "What will you help her with?"

He shrugged. "Probably the usual. An evil spirit or a bad haunting. Banishing the unclean from the house. I've done it so many times it's like riding a bike."

She'd had enough. She'd show him unclean. It was time to let the little creep and everyone else know she was on to him.

Jinx had just stepped out of the bushes and opened her mouth to speak when a hand clamped over her mouth and dragged her backwards to the other side of the bushes, out of sight of the picnic table. She stepped down hard on her attacker's foot and bit at a finger. A familiar voice yelled, "Ow! Jinx!"

"Jackson? What are you doing?"

Jackson hopped on one foot and shook his hand.

"Well what do you expect?" she said. "You do some weird kidnap move and you don't think I'm going to fight back?"

Jackson eyed her warily, then examined the bite mark on his finger. "I can't believe you didn't draw blood."

Jinx shrugged. "Yeah, well, you're lucky. And anyway, what are you doing? And where the hell have you been?" She threw her hands on her hips and stared hard at him.

"I'm stopping you from crushing that poor kid over there."

Jinx stamped her foot. "Poor kid?! You mean the one who's been copying everything we do? Who's been making up lies about how he and his family are on the set of *Ghost*

Hunters?" Jackson raised his eyebrows. "Yeah, I did some research," Jinx continued. "He's lying about the *whole thing*. His dad is a psychologist, and his mom is a psych professor at the U. Last name's Waters. He's lying about everything, Jackson."

Jackson sighed and got the look on his face that Jinx hated.

"Don't you even—" she started.

Jackson interrupted her. "J, there's probably a reason this kid feels like he needs to lie. Think of how miserable you must have to be to make up a whole new life." He looked over at Brian with sympathetic eyes.

Something stung Jinx, but she shrugged it off and let the outrage wash over her again. "But Jackson, we worked hard on that site. This is *my* thing, and he's trying to take over!"

Jackson turned his sympathetic eyes on her. "You know you matter with or without our website, right?" He put his hand on her shoulder.

Jinx knocked his hand off and stepped back. "It's not about that." She stepped back another half a foot. Blood rushed to her face. "Of course I know that. But it still doesn't make it right!"

She flipped around and stumbled on a root, then walked as fast as she could through the cafeteria doors. As she passed Brian, she glared at him, and a look of recognition came over his face. He went white. Jinx would find a way to get him, but right then she just needed to get away from Jackson and his insight. Or at least what he thought was his insight. What did he know?

Jinx sighed to herself as she realized he'd been exactly right. It wasn't until after school had let out that she realized Jackson never mentioned where he'd been the day before.

CHAPTER 7

Avoiding Jinx for a whole day had been nearly impossible. And how he'd managed to escape her question about why he'd ignored her calls and texts, he didn't know. But he had. And he felt relieved.

Then irritation traveled through him. He could have other friends besides Jinx!

Although a friendship with Haley would be a little complicated, he thought, because she was Jinx's enemy. Even so, Haley had the potential to be a bit *more* than a friend.

He shook his head to get rid of the thought. Jinx would kill him if she knew that he and Haley had plans to hang out. If he was dating her? He didn't know if the world could hold Jinx's anger.

Yet he'd been thrilled all day. At one point during school, Jackson saw Haley in the hallway and they shared a secret look. It made Jackson shiver. Not only was she beautiful, she also had a depth to her that he could now see. Behind that cheerleader outfit and the fake laugh (which Jinx had imitated more than once, and even Jackson had to laugh at) was a person with some soul.

Not to mention, she was seriously pretty.

He tried to concentrate the rest of the day at school, but all that kept running through his mind were the numbers eleven and forty-five. Finally, the bell rang and Jackson headed home. All he had to do was wait seven more hours.

Jackson's pants caught on a rough patch of bark, but he pulled his leg up to the next limb.

Haley poked her head out of a nearby window. "You're almost there," she whispered. "I can grab the bag now if you want."

Jackson nodded and arced the bag over and up so that Haley could reach it. She caught it on the first grab. She grinned down at him, her long, strawberry-blonde hair swinging below her chin. Thoughts of Rapunzel flashed through Jackson's mind, but the reality of his precarious position in the tree made him quickly shuffle the rest of the way up. Haley backed away from the window as Jackson swung his legs over the sill and stood up.

Haley's room had changed since seventh grade. Where a canopy bed filled with stuffed animals had once stood lay a chic bed with a dark wooden frame and a Moroccan-style headboard. The room was no longer drowned in pink—teals and browns, rusty reds and mustard yellows had replaced the old shades. In short, the room had grown up. Looking at Haley, Jackson thought she had too.

Candles burned in every corner of the room. On the floor, in the center, was a circle made of scarves. Two candles burned inside the circle.

Haley seemed shy, and Jackson felt the same way. They stared at each for a minute before Haley cleared her throat and put the bag with the Ouija board on the bed. She opened it and took the board out.

Handing the package to Jackson, she said, "Do you want to do the honors? It's officially yours."

Jackson smiled and said, "Sure."

He opened the package while Haley moved closer to him, peeking at the board.

A sun and moon decorated the two upper corners. Below that were the words *yes* and *no*. The alphabet and numbers were below that, right underneath the words *Good Bye*. Jackson felt Haley shiver just a little, and he fought the urge to put his arm around her. He was suddenly aware of how good she smelled. Her hair brushed his arm softly, and he felt goose bumps rise on his arms.

"Wow," Haley said.

All Jackson could do was nod. He took out the planchette, a triangular pointer with a magnifying glass in the middle. He turned it around in his hands.

"Are we supposed to see where this points or look through the glass?" he asked Haley.

She shrugged. "I have no idea. I guess we can do both and see if any of it makes sense."

"Yeah, that sounds good," Jackson said. "Do you have a pad and paper? Let's take down everything that happens."

Haley nodded and grabbed a pink pad of notepaper and a pink pen. *So not everything has completely changed with her*, Jackson thought. They looked at each other, and Jackson said, "Well, here goes nothing."

Haley and Jackson sat opposite each other in the circle. They put the board down in the middle and moved the candles to either side of it. Haley looked beautiful in the candlelight, Jackson thought, her already luminous eyes bigger and sparkly.

"Do you want to start?" Haley whispered.

Jackson swallowed and whispered back, "Sure. I mean, if you don't want to."

She smiled and shook her head. He had no

idea why they were whispering, but it seemed like the right thing to do.

Jackson placed the planchette in the middle of the board. He'd done some research on how to use the board, but all he really took away was that he needed to talk to the room, asking for the spirit to come, while he and whoever else put their hands on the planchette. Evidently the spirit would spell out what it wanted to say.

He swallowed. For some reason he felt too vulnerable to ask for his dad. "Should we do a test run tonight?" Jackson asked. "Just see if we can summon *any* spirits?"

Haley's eyes widened. "That's a really good idea. I don't think I'm quite ready . . ." Jackson nodded. He understood completely. If it didn't work, the hope would be gone again.

"OK," he said and took a deep breath. Feeling silly, he said aloud, "If there are any spirits in the room, will you make your presence known?"

Haley and Jackson both looked at their fingers on the planchette. He could feel the heat from them, they were so close. And she smelled so good . . . He waited for a minute, but nothing happened.

Jackson looked at Haley's clock. It was midnight—the shopkeeper had said that was the best time to do this sort of thing.

He cleared his throat and said again, "If there are any spirits who wish to talk to us, please use this board to communicate."

Haley added, louder, "We want to hear from you."

The planchette under their fingers trembled, and Jackson and Haley looked wild-eyed at each other.

Then they both burst out laughing as they realized it had been moved by a truck rumbling along the road outside. They quieted their laughs so her parents wouldn't hear them.

"Looks like a truckload of spirits want to talk to us," Jackson said, his fingers still on the planchette.

Haley giggled more. "They just keep trucking along."

"I'm thinking this board isn't going to give us anything tonight," Jackson added.

Haley moved her fingers until they were touching Jackson's. "Well, maybe just not what we expected."

Jackson looked into her eyes, felt the heat of her hands, saw her hair glint in the light, and then couldn't seem to stop staring at her lips. He leaned forward slowly, without thinking. Haley did the same.

When their lips finally met, before the last thought had run from Jackson's mind, it dawned on him that the board was worth every penny.

CHAPTER 8

After her run-in with Jackson, Jinx had gone home and sulked on her bed. She just couldn't let the imposter get away unpunished. Let Jackson be the nice one. She never said she was.

She sat up and touched her Pixies poster for guidance.

Flipping open her laptop, she punched in the password to get her to her website. Taking a deep breath, she uploaded the pictures of Brian.

If he wanted to play, she'd play.

Under his pictures, she wrote, *FRAUD.*
THIS BOY IS NOT WHO HE SAYS HE IS.
AND I HAVE PROOF.

Then she wrote the address of the
Paranormalator's site and the phone number
too, even though it didn't work.

She hesitated to save it for a full two
minutes. Taking out a Twizzler and chewing
on it, she finally pressed post.

There. Now Brian the poser would have to
face the music.

Jinx knew it was coming. Still, she was
surprised to find herself nervous about the
whole thing.

At lunch the next day, Brian came
storming up to her picnic table, freshman
minions following close behind. *So this is*
what angry munchkins look like, thought Jinx.
Brian's face was contorted in anger, and his
hair flopped in front of his eyes. Jinx took
a bite of her peanut butter sandwich and
smiled sweetly.

"Yes?" she asked, eyebrows high. "Can I help you?"

"You!" Brian wagged his finger at her. "You *lied* on your site! You called me a fraud, when *you're* the fraud!" He ended his tirade with a flourish of his arms, then looked to his minions for agreement.

Still acting as innocent as possible, Jinx asked, "Why were you on my website? Don't you have your own?"

Brian sputtered. Out of the corner of her eye, Jinx saw Jackson in the hallway that led out to the courtyard, talking to Haley Richards. She grimaced. Jackson worked in the counseling office this period—her lunch period—so he got to roam the halls pretty much free. But what was he doing with Haley Richards? Were they laughing?

Jinx's attention snapped back to Brian. "I was checking out the competition!" he finally said. "I demand you take that down!"

Jinx started to grow tired of the game. Other people had gathered around the table to see the fight. Jinx could hear whispers and anticipation hung in the air.

Standing up, she crossed her arms and put on her meanest look. She stepped toward Brian, and he took a small step back but held her gaze.

"I did a little research, *Bri*-an. And it turns out that your dad does *not*, in fact, work for *Ghost Hunters*. You do not travel with the crew. Your parents are both psychologists, and one of them is a professor at the U. You copied every single thing on your website from mine. And you've been lying to everyone since you got here."

Brian's face had turned beet-red. He laughed a little too high. "That's ridiculous! You copied me! And how would you know about my family?"

Jinx was prepared for that too. She whipped out copies she'd made of his mom's bio from the university website, complete with a picture of her and her family—Brian included.

He took a copy, and his eyes bugged out. Across the crowd that had gathered, small giggles had started to break out. Brian's freshman minions stared at him in betrayal and shock. Jinx felt the urge to laugh herself.

She stepped closer to Brian, who was still holding the piece of paper in front of him like he couldn't believe his eyes. "Now that's how you conduct an investigation," she said softly.

Then she flipped around and reached in her bag for business cards. Throwing them in the air over the crowd, she said, "Here's the real deal!"

Cards rained from the air, and people grabbed them, laughing and bumping into each other.

A pretty good day, Jinx thought to herself.

CHAPTER 9

When Jackson glanced out the windows of the cafeteria and saw the crowd with Jinx in the middle, his heart sank.

He turned to Haley. "I think I need to check this out."

She flipped her hair and looked outside. "Yeah, that doesn't look good." Then she smiled up at him, and he couldn't help but smile back.

He squeezed her arm. Just her touch sent a tingle up his spine. "I'll call you later on tonight," he said.

Haley smiled and nodded, then leaned in quick to give him a peck on the cheek. She walked away so fast Jackson couldn't respond.

He rubbed his cheek for a second, smelling the perfume she left behind. Then movement caught his eye. Outside, Jinx had just flipped a ton of business cards in the air. She stood atop the picnic table as kids scrambled to get them. Jackson had to laugh.

But then he saw the Brian kid.

Red-faced and shaking, Brian stormed away in the middle of the clamor. Nobody noticed him go.

Jackson's heart sank. He was sure Jinx had just confronted Brian. And probably in a really public and humiliating way. For a moment, irritation swept over Jackson. He was always putting people together after Jinx had torn them apart. Then he saw Brian head around a corner, and he took off after the kid before he lost his trail.

Jackson didn't have to go far. On the other side of the bushes, a crying Brian sat shaking only feet away from the picnic table.

But hardly anyone turned that corner in the courtyard, so really, he was a world away.

Brian looked up in surprise at Jackson and sniffled hurriedly. "Allergies. Wanted to get away from that crowd before I sneezed on everyone."

Jackson sighed, then sat down next to him. "Dude," was all he said.

Brian nodded and hung his head. He pulled up his knees and started crying again. After a minute, Jackson asked, "You want to talk about it?"

Brian shrugged, then took a swipe at his still-sniffling nose and exhaled loudly. Picking up a piece of grass, he kept his eyes trained on it as he twisted it to shreds.

"This is my fourth move in four years," he said to Jackson. "My last school . . . well, let's just say I wasn't exactly popular."

Jackson nodded. He and Jinx had something in common there.

"So this year I wanted to make a big impression. And I started researching Portland and came across your site. I thought it was wicked cool." He smiled at Jackson.

Jackson shook his head and smiled too. "That's all Jinx, man. She's amazing at that stuff. The graphics and setup? It was all her."

"Yeah, it really is." Brian said. "I mean that, even though she just shredded me out there."

Jackson could tell by looking at the boy's brown eyes that he really did mean it. He truly admired Jinx.

"Anyway, I decided I'd do the same thing. I just figured that no one probably knew about your site anyway, and if I came in I could just sort of take over that niche. I didn't count on Jinx being so . . ."

Jackson raised his eyebrows. "Protective?"

Brian looked sideways. "Sure. That word could be used to describe her."

Jackson chuckled a little, and the boys fell silent for a few seconds.

Then Brian said, "I have something else to confess. I wrote to you guys about a haunting. This was after I made the website."

Jackson's eyebrows couldn't have gone any farther up his head. "You're Mayhem?"

Brian nodded.

"But didn't you say you were in eighth grade?" Jackson asked. Even though he'd been avoiding Jinx, he still read the e-mails their potential client had sent her.

"Yeah, well, since I had already made a website saying I was *the* ghost hunter in town, I couldn't exactly tell the truth, could I? So when Jinx wrote me back . . . I had to get her off my trail. But she's . . ."

"Persistent?" Jackson said.

Brian said, "Sure."

"So, do you really have a haunting?"

Brian turned fully toward Jackson. "That's the thing, man. I really do. I can't get rid of it. And it only happens when I'm alone in the house."

Jackson shivered. How creepy was that? "Well, you really should hire us."

Brian looked at him like he was crazy. "Jinx will murder me. Then she'll murder my ghost."

Jackson rubbed his chin. "I don't think so. I mean, I'll talk to her, and I'll come with you to tell the story. But I think the possibility of a real case will override her sense of injustice. Plus, maybe you can both apologize to each other."

Brian nodded glumly. "When should we do this meeting then?"

Jackson stood up, grinning. "No time like the present!"

Brian went white and groaned.

CHAPTER 10

When Jinx got in the car, she was already talking. ". . . should have seen it, Jackson. Cards raining down like magic and that creep gone—"

She glanced into the backseat, and Jackson watched her stiffen at the sight of the exact creep she'd been talking about. Jinx turned to Jackson and glared her meanest glare. He knew because he'd seen all of her mean glares. This one was definitely the meanest.

"What. Is. He. Doing. Here?" She turned the glare onto Brian, who seemed to shrink away.

"I told you this wasn't a good idea, dude," Brian murmured.

"Yeah, that's the understatement of the year." Jinx folded her arms and looked at Jackson.

"J, will you just do me this favor and hear him out?"

Jinx sighed so heavily Jackson was afraid the vibrations would shatter the windows. But he also knew that she felt she owed him one after their first official case had revealed some trust issues on Jinx's part.

She glared at him one more time, then shifted to Brian, eyebrows raised and lips set in a taut line.

"Talk."

Brian was so startled that he immediately jumped into almost exactly what he'd told Jackson. When he was finished, he added, "And I'm really sorry."

Jackson studied Jinx's face. He knew that look. She felt bad for the kid and was trying to hide it. He even would have guessed that she felt bad about outing him at school.

"So these things only happen when you're alone in the house?" she asked.

Brian nodded. "Yeah, it's so weird. Things fly around and break, and then my parents come home and think that I did it. It's awful. They say they don't even know me now." He hung his head again, and Jackson felt a pang of sadness for him. Brian's loneliness wafted from him like it was a physical thing.

Jinx twisted her lip. "Is there a time when your parents are going out of town soon?"

Brian shook his head. "I don't think so."

She smiled mischievously. "Well, maybe they could win something soon."

Both Jackson and Brian looked at her. "What?" they asked at the same time.

Jinx rummaged through her backpack and grabbed her phone. "Jackson, don't start driving yet," she said.

"OK." Jackson shrugged.

"You got a home phone? One that *works*? And are your parents around right now?" Jinx asked Brian.

"Oh, yeah. I made that phone number up on the flyer. I didn't actually want people to call." At Jinx's hard stare he went on, hurriedly, "Uh, what day is it? Thursday, right?" he asked. "Yeah, actually, they should be. My dad works in the mornings, and my mom doesn't have class today. Why?" His expression turned suspicious.

"What's the *number*? A real one this time."

"*Why?*"

Jinx just glared at him. He sighed. "555-3847."

She punched in the numbers, and Jackson could hear ringing. A woman's voice answered on the other line.

"Hello, is this Dr. Waters?" Jinx paused. "Well, I'm from the Ramada Inn downtown, and I wanted to tell you that you won the business card raffle! You and a guest can stay in the penthouse suite for one night this upcoming weekend."

Jinx was quiet for a minute, listening, then said a few uh-huhs. "Well, someone sure did, because you won right here," she explained cheerily. "Well, I'm sorry, ma'am, but this weekend is the only time to redeem this special prize. Can I go ahead and confirm you'll be joining us?"

She hung up her phone and looked at Brian. "I hope the penthouse is open . . . I probably should have checked that first." She shrugged. "Anyway, Jackson and I will come over Friday night and see what's going on. But you have to call the Ramada and book that room."

Jackson looked out the window but didn't say anything. He was supposed to go out with Haley on Friday. This was going to be tricky.

Brian looked at Jinx with wide eyes. "How am I supposed to book a hotel room? And what if it's not available?"

Jinx shrugged. "You'll figure it out. You're pretty crafty yourself, from what I've seen." She grinned at him. And for the first time since Jackson had talked to him, Brian grinned back.

CHAPTER 11

Jinx checked her equipment bags once again. This time she'd told her parents she'd be staying at Haley's house. Using that name never got old.

She couldn't stop rifling through her bags. Something was off—she was out of sorts. First of all, Jackson had been weird about plans for the night. Distant and sort of vague. Something was going on with him, but she had no idea what.

But also, something was off about Brian's story. Jinx didn't think he was lying—she just felt she was missing something that would make everything else fall into place.

Oh well, she thought. *Tonight at least one mystery is gonna get solved.*

And if she could help it, she'd get to the bottom of the Jackson mystery as well. She could be persistent if she had to be.

A car honked outside. Jinx grabbed her gear, yelled a hasty goodbye to her parents, and rushed for the door.

But her brother, Slime, stood in front of it, blocking her escape.

"Move," she said, shoving her bag into his skinny stomach.

"Ow. And no." He narrowed his eyes and grinned an evil grin. "I wanna know where you're going."

"To a friend's house."

Slime's eyes lit up. "See, that's the thing. You don't have friends! So I know you're doing something else. And I'm going to find out." He paused for what Jinx imagined he thought was dramatic effect. "Or I'm going to tell."

She used her bag to move him physically

from the door. "You're crazier than normal tonight, Slime."

As she shut the door, she heard him say, "I'm going to find out!"

Worry pecked at her. Slime could be persistent, too. And if he had got a whiff that she wasn't telling the truth, could her parents know as well?

Nah. Slime was motivated, that's all. Her parents wanted her to have friends, so they would believe these stories for a while. Still, she didn't want to get too comfortable. In the future she'd have to be a little more creative than just picking random girls' names for her alibi.

She got to the car and threw her gear in. Jackson smiled at her—a weird, dreamy sort of smile. His cheeks were flushed.

She stared at him. "Are you on drugs?"

That seemed to snap him out of whatever trance he was in. "No," Jackson snorted. He backed out of the driveway and continued to Brian's house.

During the drive, he was unusually quiet. Jinx stared at him for a while and then finally said, "What the hell is—"

At that moment, Jackson pulled into a driveway on Mohawk Avenue. "We're here!" he said and jumped out of the car. Jinx stared up at the house. It was an old Victorian home with a roof that sent shadows over the lawn. The moon hung above the place like it was setting the stage for a murder. Every room in the house was dark except for one faint light in the front. She shivered a little. No wonder this Brian guy was lonely. If she lived in such a huge house pretty much by herself . . . Especially one that looked so dark and foreboding . . . She grabbed her gear and petted her new infrared camera through the duffel bag. It was going to be a good night—spooky house and all.

Brian greeted them at the door and smiled hugely. "I'm so excited for this!"

Jinx and Jackson looked at each other as they went into the house. Jinx wondered what he was excited about. Finding the ghost? Getting rid of the ghost? Or just having company?

"I did a lot of research when I was, um, setting up my site, and this stuff is so cool!" Brian continued. "I even bought an EVP monitor."

Jinx dropped her stuff. "Ooh! What kind?"

"Well, I splurged and got the Spirit Box?"

Jinx stopped in her tracks. "Are you kidding me? I've wanted one of those—" She cut herself off and said, "Guess what I just got? My parents bought me an infrared cam."

Brian's eyes got huge. "You have got to be joking. No way!"

Jinx nodded big. "I know, right?! They're so expensive, but my mom just got this new position at work—"

Jackson interrupted, "Your mom got a new job?"

"Yes, dumb-dumb, and you'd know that if you answered any of my texts."

All of a sudden, Jackson was all business. "Well, let's set up and wait. Does it usually happen at night, Brian?"

Brian scratched his hair. "It happens randomly, I guess. So it might not happen at all."

Jinx set up the tripod in the corner, setting her brand-new camera carefully on the holder. She had to stop herself from kissing it. She looked through the lens to make sure it was pointed in the right direction. Afterward, she took out the EVP device and set it on the table, then turned on her EMF device. "Well, it wouldn't be the first time we waited for nothing, that's for sure."

Brian kept talking. "It's so weird, but our last house was haunted, too. We seem to be attracted to haunted houses."

Jinx thought he was lucky. She'd kill for a ghost at her place. She did one more check to make sure that everything was set and then looked at the DVD collection near the TV.

"We could always watch a movie while we wait. It's not like it would scare the ghosts."

Jackson and Brian both nodded enthusiastically.

Before either boy could speak, Jinx yelled, "I get first pick!"

"This isn't a movie," Jackson grumbled.

Jinx munched on popcorn happily. "No, it's better than a movie."

Brian smiled. "I thought I was the only *Veronica Mars* fan. It's so old I didn't think anyone else knew about it. Guess not."

Jackson huffed, and Jinx looked at him curiously. He kept texting someone on his phone, and Jinx was about to ask when Brian started talking.

"I love Veronica's dad. I love the relationship she has with him."

Jinx threw more popcorn in her mouth and nodded. "I know. They do a good job with that."

Brian was quiet for a minute. Then he said quietly, "At least he knows Veronica exists."

A loud bump sounded in the hallway. Jackson and Jinx both jumped. Brian's face had turned stormy, and he didn't seem to notice the noise. "Do you guys have good relationships with your parents?" he continued.

Jinx, thinking she'd imagined the noise, answered him half-distracted. "Yeah. My parents are cool. Clueless, but cool." She looked at Jackson, "Did you hear that noise?"

"What about you, Jackson?" Brian asked.

Jackson looked toward the hallway too. "Yeah, I did hear it." Then he said, "I have a great relationship with my parents."

Jinx looked at him curiously. Parents? He had a great relationship with his mom, but . . .

She decided to get to the bottom of things. "Where have you been lately, Jackson?"

Jackson turned to her, eyes innocent. "What do you mean?"

"Hey guys," Brian said, "I thought we were having a conversation here?"

Jinx went on like Brian hadn't spoken. "I mean, you've been ignoring my calls and texts, acting strange. What is going on with you?"

"So I have to check in with you for everything?"

Jinx felt like she'd been slapped. Another bump sounded in the hall.

"Can you guys talk about this later? I thought we were here to investigate things." Brian's voice had gotten louder.

Something crashed in the hall. All three of them jumped, but Jinx wasn't done. "What the hell is that supposed to mean?" she said to Jackson, her voice loud and angry. "We're *supposed* to be best friends. Since when do you hide things from me?"

Jackson responded just as angrily. "Maybe you're hard to talk to sometimes! Did you think of that?"

"Guys . . ." Brian murmured.

"What is it you can't talk to me about, Jackson?" Jinx yelled back. She was standing up and so was Jackson. They glared at each other, face-to-face.

All of a sudden, the DVD case shot across the room.

"Uh-oh," Brian said. He looked to Jackson and Jinx. "Duck."

CHAPTER 12

Jackson tackled Jinx to the floor as magazines, coasters, and remote controls flew through the air. Brian army-crawled over to them.

Jinx smacked Jackson and hissed, "Get off, get off!" He leaned back and let go of her. For a minute, her smell lingered in his nose—Twizzlers and some brand of shampoo he couldn't place.

"I told you," Brian said.

Just as fast as the stuff had started flying,

all the magazines and coasters fell down. Like the gravity in the room had turned back on. The three of them stood up slowly and surveyed the damage.

Jinx ran over to her new piece of equipment, put her hand on her chest, and breathed out. The camera was fine.

The living room, however, was not.

Everything was scattered around, the remote controls broken, paper shredded, even throw pillows thrown. Jackson couldn't believe the mess.

"Does it happen more than once a night?" Jinx asked.

Brian shrugged glumly. "Not normally. That was a pretty typical instance."

Jinx glared at Jackson. "Then I think I'll take the equipment home and see what happened," she said.

Brian looked crushed. "You guys aren't staying the night?"

Jinx shook her head.

Jackson sighed angrily. He normally never fought back with Jinx—it was pointless. But this time felt different. This time he'd cut his date with Haley short to work a case. For Jinx.

He stuffed equipment into his bag and said, "Fine. Thanks for dragging me over here, Jinx. Per usual, all you think about is yourself."

Jinx turned around. "I'll call my dad for a ride home," she yelled. "Then *you* won't have to think of me any longer."

Jackson glared at her. "Fine!"

Jinx glared back. "Fine!"

Jackson stomped out the door, leaving a bewildered Brian standing among pieces of shredded magazines.

It wasn't until the following Monday that Jackson heard from Jinx. He'd meant to call—he hated fighting with her—but something kept him from doing it. And he'd been spending a lot of time with Haley. A lot of time. In fact, they'd decided they were dating, something that thrilled Jackson to his core. And, for many reasons, also completely terrified him.

Jinx found Jackson on her lunch break, in the middle of his counseling-office roamings.

She walked up to him and said, "Truce?"

Jackson sighed. "Truce. What'd you find out about the haunting?"

Jinx leaned in, totally engaged, completely excited. Every once in a while Jinx opted not to hold a grudge. Jackson was thrilled that this was one of those times. "That's the thing, I didn't see anything. Not a thing. I mean, the camera caught the stuff being thrown around, but there was *no* other evidence of a ghost. Nothing on the EVP or EMF."

Jackson's face scrunched up. "But there was clearly activity. I mean, the living room was trashed!"

Jinx gave him a dirty look. "Yeah, I know. And I had to help clean it up while I waited for my dad."

Jackson felt a pang of guilt. He thought maybe now would be a good time to tell her about Haley. In the hallway. In public.

"Jinx, I—"

She waved her hand impatiently. "Never mind that. I think what we have on our hands here is a poltergeist phenomenon."

Jackson looked at her quizzically.

"Remember in our last case, when I thought that's what might be it?" Jinx continued. "With the brothers fighting? Well, this one *totally* fits the description. And remember, Brian said his last house was haunted, too! And, it only happens when he's home alone."

Jackson nodded. "The poltergeist thing is when someone is so upset they create paranormal activity in the house, right? But it's not a haunting?"

"Exactly. And it's almost always adolescents. And if Brian has had this happen for a while . . ."

Jackson sighed. "He told me this is his fourth move in four years."

Jinx raised her eyebrows. "That'd make a person unhappy." Her eyes got wide. "And remember Friday, when it started? We talked about parents, but then you and I fought?"

Jackson said, "And Brian got upset. We spurred him into poltergeist activity!"

Jinx nodded seriously. "We need to tell him before it gets worse. I've done some research—it could get really bad. Like knives-in-the-air bad."

Jackson scanned the hall. "I'll go look for him."

"Find him," Jinx stressed and walked away.

Finding Brian wasn't hard. He was out behind the bushes again. He looked up when Jackson blocked the sun.

"We figured out what's going on." Jackson said as he sat down next to him.

Brian closed the comic book he'd been reading. "What? What kind of ghost? Can you get rid of it?"

Jackson tried to think of the nicest way possible to tell him he was the cause. "Well . . . it's not exactly a ghost. But it *can* be gotten rid of."

Brian's eyebrows rose.

"Brian, have you heard of a poltergeist?"

"Yeah," Brian said. "It's not a ghost, but a manifestation of bad energy. I read all about it when I was researching your site." He grinned at Jackson. Then comprehension dawned on his face. "Wait, you guys think that's what's going on?"

"Yeah."

"But why?"

"Well, nothing showed up on the equipment," Jackson said. "Nothing ghostly. And you said that you'd been haunted in a lot of different places, so . . ."

Brian looked away. "Yeah . . . Oh my god, I didn't even think. I can't believe I've been causing all this!"

Jackson said, "Well, the good news is you can stop it. You just need to figure out what it is you need to feel at peace."

But Brian didn't seem to be listening. "I mean, *I* caused this. Me. I made this happen." Jackson saw excitement in Brian's eyes, and it unnerved him.

"Listen, dude, Jinx researched this stuff, and it could get worse and worse. You're going to want to try to stop this."

Brian stood up and looked down at Jackson as if he were a bug. "Yeah, I'll do that," he hissed. "I have these new superpowers, and I'll just let them go."

Jackson stood up. "These aren't superpowers, Brian. This is dangerous, and you won't be able to control it. You need to find a way to stop it, not spur it on."

Brian stared at Jackson with disdain. "You're just jealous. You can't do anything like this. You're"—he spat the word at Jackson—"ordinary."

Jackson shivered as Brian stormed away. There was something seriously wrong with the boy. Something dark in him. He'd have to tell Jinx to be careful.

Jackson took out his phone to text Jinx, but then he saw Haley through the windows of the cafeteria. Every other thought left his mind. He put his phone away, not remembering why he had it out.

CHAPTER 13

Later that night, Jackson thought back to his encounter with Brian. He shuddered as the creepy look on Brian's face flashed in his mind, and he thought of the power Brian had. Brian was almost like the evil version of Jinx—refusing to be ordinary, but willing to go to dangerous extremes to get there. He had to remember to tell her. He'd call her tomorrow.

Jackson pulled up his shirt and put on deodorant. Haley was coming over; they were going to watch a movie. And maybe even try the Ouija board again. Jackson wasn't ready to give up on it yet. And the fact that Haley was a part of the effort just made the whole thing that much sweeter.

He put on a sweater and jeans and then heard the doorbell ring. He looked at his watch—Haley was about ten minutes early. But that's what he liked about her; she was very considerate.

He jogged down the stairs and opened the door.

Jinx stood there, holding popcorn and a DVD. "I thought maybe we could watch a movie. I think you'll like it," she said. "*Paranormal Activity.*"

Jackson snorted. *Paranormal Activity* was a movie that *Jinx* liked. Then he went white. He needed to get her out of there fast, before Haley came over. Before Jackson could say anything, Jinx flounced in and walked up the stairs to his room.

Jackson followed, saying, "Uh . . . actually, I have to . . ."

Jinx walked in his room and turned around, a Twizzler in her hand. "You have to what?"

Then she caught sight of the Ouija board. "Whoa!" She shoved the rest of the Twizzler in her mouth and grabbed it. "I didn't know you had one of these things! Why haven't we used it a gazillion times by now?"

She swallowed a mouthful of Twizzler and frowned. "Wait, why *do* you have one of these things? I thought you really didn't care about paranormal stuff . . . you were just doing this because it was something to do."

Jackson had opened his mouth—to say what, he didn't know—when the doorbell rang again. He stammered, "Stay here. Don't move."

"What? Why are you acting so weird? And why are you wearing a sweater?" She sniffed the air. "Is that cologne?"

"Just don't move," he said again and sprinted down the stairs.

He opened the door. Haley stood on the other side. She smiled at him, and Jackson melted just a little—before the adrenaline kicked in and sweat trickled down his spine.

"You smell good," Haley said. She handed him a bag of what felt like heavy candles and a book. "For tonight." She giggled. "Who'd have guessed I'd ever be on a date where the main event was using a Ouija board!"

Jackson heard a gagging sound on the stairway and closed his eyes. He knew Jinx had heard the whole thing.

He turned around slowly and watched as Jinx stomped down each stair until she stood by Jackson.

At the same time Haley and Jinx said, "What's she doing here?"

Jackson sighed and leaned against the doorsill. "Jinx, Haley and I are dating."

Jinx's mouth dropped open. "Her? Out of all the people in the world, Jackson . . . her?"

He started to say, "You don't know her—"

"And you've started this new Ouija board thing with *her*?" Jackson had never heard Jinx's voice go so quiet. He knew that wasn't good.

Meanwhile, Haley had crossed her arms. "Yeah. *Me*. Jackson, I thought you were just friends with her out of pity."

Haley and Jinx glared at each other with hate. "Haley," Jackson started, "Jinx is my best friend. Since kindergarten."

Jinx looked back and forth between Haley and Jackson. Jackson thought he saw tears in her eyes. "Was," she said with a husky voice. "*Was* his best friend." She pushed past Haley and out to the sidewalk.

"Jinx—" Jackson called, but Jinx flipped around and said, "You two deserve each other." She started to run.

Jackson went to follow, but Haley put her hand on his chest. "Let her go. What do you need her for? We've got each other now." She stood on her toes and gave him a quick kiss on the lips.

But all Jackson could see was the retreating form of his best friend heading down the block.

Paranormalists Blog—

Dear PF fans,

There have been some changes here. Some big ones. Actually, one big one. Investigator #2 has been removed from the Paranormalist investigation team.

What does this mean for you, loyal fans and potential customers? Nothing! I promise. We still have the best equipment and the kick-butt investigative skills you've come to expect.

And even better, I have a new assistant. Everyone, meet Brian. Brian, meet everyone.

So while things have changed on this end, really, for you, they will be the same. As always, the Paranormalists SEEK THE TRUTH AND FIND THE CAUSE.

Even if we're one short.

Sincerely,

Investigator #1

SEEK THE TRUTH
AND FIND THE CAUSE
WITH

THE PARANORMALISTS

CASE 1:
THE HAUNTING OF APARTMENT 101
Jinx was a social reject who became a punked-out paranormal investigator. Jackson is a jock by day and Jinx's ghost-hunting partner by night. When a popular girl named Emily asks the duo to explore a haunting in her dad's apartment, Jinx is skeptical—but Jackson insists they take the case. And the truth they find is even stranger than Emily's story.

CASE 2:
THE TERROR OF BLACK EAGLE TAVERN
Jinx's ghost-hunting partner Jackson may be a jock, but Jinx is not interested in helping his football buddy Todd—until Todd's case gets too weird to ignore. A supernatural presence is causing chaos at the bar Todd's family owns. And the threat has a connection to Todd that's deeper than even he realizes . . .

CASE 3:
THE MAYHEM ON MOHAWK AVENUE
Jinx and Jackson have become the go-to ghost hunters at their high school. When a new kid in town tries to get in on their business, Jinx is furious. Portland only needs one team to track down ghosties! But Jinx's quest to shut down her competition will lead her and Jackson down a dangerous path . . .

CASE 4:
THE BRIDGE OF DEATH
Jinx is the top paranormal investigator at her high school, and she has a blog to prove it. Jackson's her ghost-hunting partner by night—former partner, anyway. After a shakeup in the Paranormalists' operation, the two ex-best friends are on the outs, and at the worst possible time. Because a deadly supernatural threat is putting their classmates in harm's way . . .

AFTER THE DUST SETTLED

PLAGUE RIDERS

GABRIEL GOODMAN

FIGHT THE WIND

RIVER RUN

PIG CITY

JONATHAN MARY-TODD

SHOT DOWN

JONATHAN MARY-TODD

SNAKEBITE

JONATHAN MARY-TODD

The world is over.
Can you survive what's next?

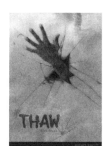

MEGAN ATWOOD

lives in Minneapolis, MN, and gets to write books for a living. She also teaches writing classes and reads as many young adult books as she can get her hands on. She only occasionally investigates paranormal activity.